A Christmas Star Called Hannah

Vivian French

illustrated by
Anne Yvonne Gilbert

CANDLEWICK PRESS
CAMBRIDGE, MASSACHUSETTS

"Come on, Mom," said Hannah, "or we'll be late for school."

"We're coming," Mom said, tucking Paul into his stroller.

Hannah gave a little skip.

"Mrs. Hill's going to tell us about a surprise today—a Christmas surprise. I think it might be gingerbread cookies."

"That's nice," said Mom.

Mrs. Hill called all the children together
at story time.

"Now," said Mrs. Hill, "we're going to put
on a Christmas play for our moms and
dads and friends. We're going to tell
them the story of Mary and Joseph and
the baby Jesus."

"Hurray!" said Hannah.

Everyone was told who or what they would be. Hannah was upset because Mrs. Hill chose Zak to be Joseph and Susie to be Mary.

Hannah was only a star. She went to sit under the table.

"This is a very special star," Mrs. Hill told her. "You'll show everyone the way to the stable."

"Policemen do that," Hannah said. "Stars just twinkle."

Mrs. Hill sighed. "This star is baby Jesus' very own star."

"Oh." Hannah thought about stars for a moment. "I'll be a star, then," she said.

Zak's mom came to help the children
paint a big picture of the inn and the
stable where the baby Jesus was born.
Susie and Roger and Aaron went to look
in the playhouse for a doll to be
the baby. Hannah came over to see
what they were doing.
"I could bring my dolly from home,"
she said. "It's much bigger than this one."
"Oh, I think this one will do, Hannah,"
said Zak's mom.

Hannah went over to the dress-up corner.
She put on a big hat, some shiny beads, and
a pair of sparkly shoes.
"I've found some things to wear,"
she said. "Look!"
Roger's mom looked at her list of names.
"Aren't you the Christmas star, Hannah?"
Hannah nodded. "These are my star clothes."
"I don't think they're quite right, dear,"
Roger's mom said. "We're going to make
you a lovely sparkly costume."
"Can't I wear the hat I found?" Hannah asked.
"No, dear," said Roger's mom.

Hannah walked home very slowly.
"I don't want to be in the play," she said.
"Plays are dumb."
"It'll be fun when you do it," said her
mom. "Paul and I are both coming
to watch."
"Paul will probably cry and spoil it,"
Hannah said crossly.

On the day of the play, all the moms and dads and friends packed into the auditorium. The children put on their costumes and peered out through the curtains.

"I can see my mom and Paul," said Hannah.

"Is everybody ready?" Mrs. Hill asked. "Susie, have you got the doll wrapped up, ready to be baby Jesus?"

Susie stared at Mrs. Hill. Then she began to cry.

"I forgot it," she sobbed.

Jamie's dad began to play the piano.
"We'll just have to pretend that we have a
baby Jesus," Mrs. Hill said, quickly wiping
Susie's nose. "Don't cry, Susie."
"I know what!" Hannah jumped down from
her bench. "I have a baby to be Jesus!"
She burst through the curtains and rushed
down the hall. A moment later she was
back, pushing Paul in his stroller.
"There," Hannah said proudly, "now we
have a *real* baby!"

Mrs. Hill looked very anxious, but Susie
and Zak were already pushing the
stroller carefully across the stage to the
stable. Roger's mom pulled the curtains
wide open, and Hannah stood high up on
her bench and shone happily over Paul.

At the end, everyone clapped and clapped and said it was the best play ever. Mrs. Hill gave Hannah a big hug.

"Well done, Hannah," she said, "your baby brother was perfect."

Hannah climbed down from her bench.

"I was a very special Christmas star, wasn't I?" she said.

"Yes, dear," said Mrs. Hill, "you were the best Christmas star ever!"